DRAGON STORM

Cara and Silverthief

DRAGON STORM

Cara and Silverthief

ALASTAIR CHISHOLM

nosy
crow

First published in the UK in 2022 by Nosy Crow Ltd
The Crow's Nest, 14 Baden Place,
Crosby Row, London SE1 1YW

Nosy Crow and associated logos are trademarks
and/or registered trademarks of Nosy Crow Ltd

Text © Alastair Chisholm, 2022
Cover illustration © Ben Mantle, 2022
Inside illustrations © Eric Deschamps, 2022

The right of Alastair Chisholm, Ben Mantle, and Eric Deschamps to be
identified as the author and illustrators of this work has been asserted.

ISBN: 978 1 83994 006 4

A CIP catalogue record for this book is available from the British Library

Printed and bound in Great Britain by Clays Ltd, Elcograf S.p.A.

Papers used by Nosy Crow are made from wood grown in sustainable forests.

IN THE LAND OF DRACONIS, THERE ARE NO DRAGONS.

Once, there were. Once, humans
and dragons were friends, and guarded
the land. They were wise, and strong, and
created the great city of Rivven together.

But then came the Dragon Storm, and
the dragons retreated from the world
of humans. To the men and women of
Draconis, they became legends and myth.

And so, these days, in the land of Draconis,
there are no dragons…

…Or so people thought.

THE SILVER THIEF

In the dead dark of a moonless night, a young girl climbed the palace walls.

The palace stood on an ancient rock that rose high above the city of Rivven. Its walls were well made, of smooth grey stone with few handholds, but the girl moved confidently, ignoring the drop below her. Finding a crack between two bricks, she pulled herself up and placed her feet against a thin ledge. She reached for the next gap.

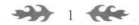

DRAGON STORM,

Wait.

The voice came from inside her head. She didn't know how, or whose voice it was, but she'd heard it her whole life. It was her only friend, and she trusted it. She stopped. Above her, a guard leaned out over the edge of the wall and gazed down, bored. The figure waited, hidden in a grey cloak that perfectly matched the stonework, until the guard wandered away.

Now, said the voice.

She continued climbing until she came to a narrow window about halfway up, then squeezed through and into a corridor, landing in a crouch. No one was around. Faint torchlight flickered at one end, and a solid wooden door blocked the other.

She removed her cloak and tucked it into her backpack. Underneath, she was a small, thin girl, with silver-blonde hair and a pinched, serious face. She wore dark colours, mottled like shadows. She crept towards the door and listened for a moment, and then slowly lifted the latch and entered.

Beyond were more corridors, some dark, some lit by torchlight. She moved cautiously. At one point she stopped and sank into the shadows as a servant scurried past. The floor had rich-red carpet now, and torches burned in alcoves.

On the left, said the voice.

The girl paused. The patch of wall to her left seemed different, the stonework slightly pale. She felt round the edges until she was sure, then pushed at one brick …

… and the wall swung outwards, revealing a hidden entrance.

The girl's face didn't change. She crept into the darkness along a narrow passageway, feeling her way until she reached another doorway, opened it, and entered a room.

Inside it was bright, and shimmering with lamplight, and *rich*. Every inch shone with precious metal, dark polished wood, crystal. Beautiful embroideries covered the walls, shimmering with golden thread. In the middle of the room sat a huge four-poster bed.

This is it, said the voice. *King Godfic's royal quarters!*

The girl stared around, her mouth open.

Come on, we'd better be quick.

She nodded, and tiptoed across to a grand dressing table in front of an enormous mirror.

He likes looking at himself, doesn't he?

The girl grinned and checked the drawers. One was full of little jars of powder and perfume; one held a display of embroidered lace handkerchiefs. One had papers, and wax, and the king's official stamp.

One was locked. The girl pulled two pins from her hair and carefully used them to feel inside the lock. Then she *twisted*, and the lock clicked. She slid the drawer open … and gasped.

The inside was lined with dark-red velvet, and its contents shimmered. There were gold and silver rings, a heavy gold link necklace, a chain of pearls. Beautiful, ornate pins carved into the shapes of animals, inlaid with precious stones. Coins lay scattered at the base. And in the centre, on its own stand, sat a large golden brooch with an enormous diamond.

That's it!

Carefully, the girl picked up the brooch and peered at it. Its base was an octagon, with eight ornate golden sides, framing a

Cara and Silverthief

diamond that shone like a star. There was something in the diamond's heart – perhaps painted underneath? Peering inside, she made out an eye, beautifully drawn, fierce, and somehow cruel. Not a human eye; more like a cat's, or a wolf's, or…

I don't like that.

"What?" The girl was surprised. "It's just a picture."

It's creepy.

She shrugged, and looked back – and the eye moved.

"Argh!" she yelled, dropping it. The eye glanced around, and then straight at her, and blinked! And suddenly a bell started tolling from the corridor outside, hard and fast and sharp.

You've triggered an alarm!

"It moved!" she hissed.

I know! Forget it! Come on!

There were other noises now, shouts and running footsteps. The girl ran back to the far wall and the secret passage, closing it behind her just as she heard someone at the main door.

She fumbled through the black corridor, trying to stay quiet. Would they know about the hidden entrance? She reached the end of the passage and pushed the door open a crack. The corridor was empty, and she hurried back to where she'd come in, dragging her cloak and a grappling rope from her bag. She poked her head through the slit window, then pulled it back sharply and cursed. There were guards all along the top of the wall now, holding lanterns and staring hard.

We can't go that way – they'll see us!

The girl felt panic rise inside her.

Boots thundered behind her. More guards! She raced towards the brighter end of the corridor, back into the depths of the palace.

What are we going to do?

She kept moving, glancing around. There were rooms on either side – could she sneak into one of them? The alarm bells clanged and a guard shouted, "You check that way!"

What are we going to DO, Cara?

And then a black-gloved hand reached from a doorway, covered her mouth, and dragged her backwards. The door closed behind her and someone pinned her arms and whispered harshly in her ear.

"Be quiet."

STREET RAT

"Be quiet."

It was a man's voice, and he was strong, pinning down Cara's arms. *"Don't move."*

Cara snorted. She lifted her feet and slammed both heels *hard* against the side of one kneecap. The man cursed and half collapsed, and she prised herself free and reached for the door—

"Wait!"

At the last moment she heard boots in the

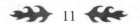

corridor. *Guards!* She looked back at the man, now clutching his knee in pain. He held a finger to his lips. "Shh!"

Cara hesitated, and waited for the footsteps to fade away.

The man nodded. "It was the tower watch," he said. "They always come this way. They're looking for you."

He was young, dressed in dark clothes, with curly black hair and a friendly expression. An old, faded scar marked one side of his face. Cara glanced around warily. They were in a small room, simple but clean. A thin bed rested against one wall, a table and chair at the other, with several candles, an inkwell, long feather pens, and neat piles of paper.

The man stood, wincing and rubbing his knee. "Good move, by the way. Daisy would be impressed." He held out a hand. "I'm Malik."

Cara didn't know who Daisy was. She ignored him and turned back to the door.

"You won't be able to climb down the wall, you know."

She stopped.

"I saw you climb up," he said. "Very impressive! But they're watching now; they'll see you if you try to get down that way."

Cara knew he was right. What was she going to do?

"I know another way," he said. "I can get you out."

She scowled. "Why would I trust you?"

Malik shrugged. "I could have shouted for the guards. You're a street rat, aren't you?"

She didn't answer.

He nodded. "No parents. Nowhere to live, surviving on the streets. On your wits. That was me once. I was like you. I admit, I stole the odd apple myself, when I had to." Then he laughed. "Nothing like this though! What on earth were you looking for, sneaking into the palace?"

Cara said nothing, but he didn't seem to

mind. "These days I do something different," he said.

Cara looked again at the quills and paper. "A clerk."

"Yes … but something else, too. I look for people." His voice changed. Suddenly he seemed more serious. "Special people. Ones who see things others don't. A face in the fire, maybe?"

Cara frowned. What was he talking about?

We should go, said the voice in her head.

She nodded and reached for the door handle.

"Or perhaps hear things?" called Malik.

Cara stopped and looked back. "What?"

Malik nodded. "People who hear things

others can't," he said quietly. "Like a voice, always there. Knowing things you don't. Helping you."

How can he know that, Cara?

Cara shook her head.

Malik smiled. "As soon as I saw you, I could tell. It's like a *glow*, you know?" She said nothing. "Would you like to know what it is?"

Slowly, Cara released the handle. The corridor outside was empty. She should go, she knew.

"Would you like to see whose voice it is?" asked Malik.

What's he talking about, Cara? What does he mean, "whose voice"?

Cara chewed her lip. Then she gave a very short nod.

Malik grinned. "Great! Um…" He picked up one of the lit candles. "Right. I'm not very good at this, but I can show you for a moment. Watch the flame."

Warily, Cara watched it, flickering and glowing. It seemed quite normal.

The man moved his other hand in a complex pattern, muttering.

I don't like this, said the voice. *He's trying to trick you!*

But Cara watched the flame, and it stretched, filling the room with warm yellow light. And within it, she realised … she could see something. A face with a sharp chin, glowing eyes, familiar somehow…

"There," whispered Malik.

Cara glanced up – and jumped! There, in the corner, faint as a ghost, stood a large creature, with long ears, a catlike face, glowing green eyes. The body was hard to make out; it seemed to shift and change

colour. Cara stepped back, ready to run! But the face…

"Is that—" She stopped. "Is that *you*?"

"I don't know," said the voice. And Cara gasped. It wasn't in her head any more – it was coming from the creature! It stared down at itself and then back to Cara.

It held up one claw, pale and ghostly.

"What is this?" it said, astonished. "What's going on?"

"I can't bring her completely into this world," said Malik. "You'll need Drun's help for that. But this is what she looks like."

The creature gazed into Cara's face. "Cara, I think this is … I think this is *me*! I think…" It stopped. "*Silverthief*," it murmured. "That's my name. *Silverthief*. Cara, I think I'm a—"

And then a fist hammered against the door and an angry voice shouted, "Open up in there! Open in the name of the king!"

THE GUILD

"Open in the name of the king!"

Cara gasped and stared at the door. Behind her, Malik blew out the candle. "Sorry, Silverthief," he muttered. Cara turned back to see the creature's image fading away like smoke.

"Cara, what's happening?" it hissed, and then it was gone – but a moment later Cara heard the familiar voice in her mind.

Cara! That was me! I think that was me!

Cara shook her head and tried to concentrate. How could she escape? The tiny slit window in this room was too small, and there was nowhere to hide…

Malik walked towards the door. "Coming!"

"No!" hissed Cara, but he winked and reached for the handle. At the last moment, Cara flattened herself against the wall behind the door as Malik swung it open wide.

"Captain Hork!" he said, beaming.

Cara tried not to breathe. She peered out through a sliver of gap in the wood and saw a group of soldiers, and a large, sweating man with a sour expression, badly fitting bronze armour and a ridiculous plumed helmet. She knew Captain Hork. He was captain of the

King's Guard, a bully and a fool. Her heart pounded.

"What can I do for you?" asked Malik.

Captain Hork gaped. "Don't you hear the alarm?" he snarled. "The king's been robbed! Have you seen anyone acting suspiciously?"

"Gosh," said Malik, looking shocked. "How *awful*! No, sorry. But … someone *did* just run past my door. Someone big and fierce, it sounded like! He went that way." He pointed down the corridor.

"*Right*," snapped Hork, adjusting his helmet. "Next time, pay a bit more attention, eh? The king's life could be at stake!"

He paused, and seemed to think. "Big and fierce, you say?"

Malik nodded. "*Very.*"

"Hmm. Right. Er … lead on, men! I'll, er, guard the rear."

The soldiers ran off with Captain Hork bellowing after them and keeping a safe distance behind.

Malik waited until Hork's voice faded and then closed the door. "That should keep them busy," he chuckled.

Cara breathed out. She glanced at the corner of the room, but the strange creature had vanished. "Where did it go?" she asked.

"Back to her world," said Malik. "I can't summon her properly. You'll need Drun for that."

"Who's Drun?"

"A friend of mine. I'd like you to meet him. And some other friends too. People who know … what it's like to be special."

He looked serious now. "Would you like to meet them?"

Cara, I think that really was me! I think…

Cara hesitated. "All right." She frowned. "But what was it? That creature?"

Malik smiled. "I think you've already guessed," he said. "Tell me … what do you know about dragons?"

Malik found an apprentice cloak for Cara and walked her out of the palace as his new assistant, loudly giving her instructions whenever they passed a guard. Dawn was breaking, and as they came down from the rock and into the city, a few people were moving around, setting up stalls or carting fish ready for the day's markets.

"This way," murmured Malik, steering her down an alley. Cara recognised where they were and felt her skin prickle. This was the Vennels, a dangerous part of town, and one she normally stayed clear of. She checked that she still had her knife tucked into one boot.

Cara and Silverthief

What do you know about dragons?

Cara thought about this. She knew what everyone knew. That they were ferocious and terrifying. That they destroyed crops, attacked humans. And that they were a *myth* – a made-up story of monsters that might have existed a thousand years ago, but not today. Not here.

Oh, there were stories. Cara kept to herself mostly, but sometimes, when the rain was lashing and the wind howling, she would huddle for shelter with some of the other street rats, and someone would always claim something – *My mate says he saw something flying over the West Gate. I saw something moving, and it weren't human! There was a light, not natural.*

Magic, I reckon. But it was nonsense. There were no dragons. There was no magic.

But … the eye in the jewel had moved; she was sure of it. And that thing, in Malik's study… And the voice in her mind that had always been there, for so long she had never even thought about it…

"Not everyone can see them, or hear them," said Malik as they walked. "They live in their own world. But some of us – *dragonseers* – can connect. We can see them, hear them, talk to them … even summon them into this world."

"And that's what we saw? That's what you were showing me – my … my *dragon*?"

He chuckled. "Oh yes."

He ducked down into a tiny lane between two collapsed houses, and Cara tried to keep up.

"But people would *know*," she tried. "I mean … *dragons*?"

"Well, there aren't very many these days. For centuries there were none at all, after the Dragon Storm."

"I remember that story," said Cara. "That was the war, wasn't it? Between humans and dragons. And we won, and the dragons ran away."

Malik sighed. "Good lord, what do they teach kids these days? No. It wasn't between humans and dragons, we didn't win, and they didn't run away. They just … left." He grimaced. "To be honest, I think they were disappointed with us."

He shook his head. "But now they're coming back. It's very exciting, a new generation of dragons – and a new generation of *dragonseers*. Like you. Ah, here we are!"

They had reached a plain-looking door in an old cottage, as broken-down as the others. But inside was another door, which opened into a long, snaking corridor. And then a maze of twisting passages and false doorways, far larger than the cottage. Cara tried to work out where they were, but everything looked the same, and she felt a strange movement under her feet and heard the sound of gears whirring. The corridors

were *moving*, she realised – turning as they walked.

Finally they reached a larger doorway and Malik paused. "Ready?" he asked. His eyes twinkled.

Cara frowned. "For what?"

Malik grinned. "For this!"

DRAGON STORM

In one smooth movement he swung open the door and steered her through. "Welcome to the Dragonseer Guild!"

Cara stared in astonishment. "No *way*," she managed at last.

DRAGONSEER

They were standing on a raised platform, on the edge of an enormous cavern that stretched far off into the distance. Below them were buildings and what looked like training grounds. The air was full of strange globes that hung from the roof and shone pale yellow like the early-morning sun. It was the largest place Cara had ever seen. It was *colossal*.

"This is impossible," she gasped. "There's

nowhere in the city big enough for this. Where *are* we? Are we underground?"

Malik just grinned. "Come on. Let's meet the others."

He led her down to the ground and towards a collection of huts. Cara tried not to stare as she walked through the hall. There were other people, she realised. From a training area on one side came the sounds of laughter, shouting, the clash of metal swords. A tall man in a shabby grey cloak stalked past them, nodding briefly to Malik and ignoring Cara completely. She could smell woodsmoke and breakfast.

They reached the huts and Malik asked her to wait as he slipped inside.

Cara and Silverthief

Cara gazed around.

What is all this, Cara?

The voice in her head felt like a comfort.

"I don't know," she murmured.

Malik returned with a woman, tall and kindly-looking, dressed in blue robes. She nodded to Cara. "Hello, Cara," she said. "My name is Berin. Malik has told me about you and Silverthief. I'm sure you have questions, and we'll try to answer them all. But for now … welcome to the Guild!" She gave a great warm smile and Cara found it hard not to smile back.

"So…" Cara started to say but then stopped. "It's true then? I'm a … a dragonseer?"

It sounded ridiculous. But Berin smiled again.

"Oh yes. Malik is always right about these things. You're a dragonseer. Silverthief is your dragon, and you are her human. There are dragons, Cara. There is dragon magic. It's all true."

"And the voice in my head… All this time it was … *her*?"

Cara couldn't remember her parents. She'd been living on the streets of Rivven for so long she couldn't remember anything from before. Her days were cold, hungry and dangerous, and her only friend was the mysterious voice – the voice that knew things she didn't and which seemed able to find hidden things. Together they had learned how to get by, how to find shelter, how to stay alive. The voice had been with her for so long that she'd never even thought about what it was.

"It happens, sometimes," said Berin. "At some point you connected with Silverthief, but you were so young you didn't know what you'd done, and neither did she. And she's stayed with you. You two are closer than any dragon pair we've ever met."

Cara nodded. "So what do you want from me?" she asked warily.

Berin laughed. "Nothing! The Guild is here for *you*. We can teach you how to summon Silverthief, and protect her. And we can offer you a family, in a way. You can be one of us, if you'd like."

Cara hesitated.

I don't know, said the voice – Silverthief's voice, Cara realised. *We've done all right by ourselves, Cara.*

"I can … summon her? Make her real?" Cara asked. Berin nodded. "And would I still hear her voice?"

Berin smiled. "Of course!"

"And I can leave when I like?"

"Yes."

Cara squinted at Berin and then Malik.

He nodded encouragingly.

She bit her lip. "All right. For now."

Berin clapped her hands. "Excellent! We'll get you settled, show you where your dorm room is, introduce you to some of the other children. But first…" She studied Cara. "First, there's someone I'd like you to meet. Come with me."

She brought Cara to a round building away from the other huts and introduced her to a short, cheerful man named Drun. Drun was dressed in a brown leather jerkin and trews, and had a wild grey beard.

"Pleasure t'meet you!" he said, shaking her hand. He gazed at her face and nodded.

"Oh yes. You've got the look all right. Come on in."

He led her towards to a smoky fire and told her to look into the flames.

Cara was wary – the building was dark, full of shadows cast by the fire, and she wasn't sure how to get out – but she looked, and he muttered, and the flames rose.

Cara and Silverthief

"Tell me about Silverthief," he murmured. "What does she look like?"

Cara frowned. "Don't they all look the same?"

But Drun laughed. "Oh, bless you, no. Dragons is special, miss, every one unique. It depends on the human, y'see. They all look different, they all got different abilities … and they'll all get their different powers eventually."

"Powers?"

"Oh yes. Each dragon's got one. A *special* power. One that only appears when it's most needed."

So Cara described Silverthief, and the flames rose higher again, crackling and sparking suddenly, and she felt goosebumps on her arms…

And Silverthief appeared.

For real this time: solid, not faint and ghostly. A real creature, with silvery skin and short teeth, oval green eyes and a careful, watchful face. She looked down at her body and then up at Cara, and tentatively reached out.

Cara reached back. "Silverthief?"

They touched. Real. She was *real*. Cara could feel her rough strong claws against her fingertips! She felt a shiver of excitement and Silverthief smiled, half closed her eyes like a happy cat, and purred…

"Hello, Cara."

THE NORTH RUINS

Cara still couldn't work out where the Dragonseer Guild Hall was, or how anything so large could exist, but she knew it was old. Ancient, even. The training ground and huts were new, but beyond them lay the ruins of older buildings from a different age.

Now she sat atop one of the ruined walls with Silverthief curled round her, and wondered about her new life.

That first day, the day she'd summoned

Silverthief, Drun had told her the rules.

"She can't stay forever," he'd said. "She needs your connection to keep her in this world, so when you sleep she goes back. But I reckon you'll have no problem callin' her again, eh? Good luck!"

Then Berin had shown her around the rest of the hall, the dorm rooms and the central hut where they met for meals and lessons, and had introduced her to the other children.

There was Connor, clever and a bit of a show-off; Mira, obsessed with devices and machines, and often grease-smudged; Erin, the tall, strong girl who strode everywhere and shouted a lot; quiet Kai, who studied everything he could about dragon biology;

and Ellis the explorer, constantly making maps. They'd all been friendly, but Cara wasn't used to other people and found them a bit overwhelming.

She'd met the other dragons and discovered that Silverthief was quite small, as dragons go. Rockhammer, Erin's dragon, was almost twice as big, and only Connor's strange, whiplike creature, Lightspirit, was smaller.

Cara didn't care about the other dragons. Some of the other children found summoning hard, but for Cara, finding that space in her mind and heart, creating the doorway that allowed Silverthief into her world, was as easy as breathing. The voice in her head had been her only friend for years, and now her friend was real. And life in the Guild was good – regular food, proper beds, no danger. It was perfect.

Almost perfect…

"I don't trust them."

Cara patted Silverthief's smooth, warm sides.

"I know," she said. "But they've been good to us so far."

The dragon snorted. "So far. What do they *really* want? What aren't they telling us?"

"Like what?" asked Cara, frowning.

"Like…" Silverthief flicked her tail. "Like

where this place *is*."

Cara shrugged. "I suppose they want to keep it safe."

"Hmph. And I don't like the other dragons."

Cara smiled. "I know, Silver."

"Rockhammer is *so* annoying. He's always bellowing! And Boneshadow's boring. And they keep wanting to *talk* to me." Silverthief sighed. "It was always just you and me before. I don't like it now."

Cara laughed. "You love being a dragon," she said. "And you like it when I scratch behind your ears."

"Well…" Silverthief stretched her neck, purring as Cara scratched. "Well, yes."

Cara patted her again. Silverthief's skin was faintly silver, but her colours shimmered and changed to match wherever she was, like a chameleon. Like Cara, she had the knack of keeping very, very still, until she almost disappeared.

"Cara!"

Cara looked down. Heading towards them were two of the other children, Ellis and Mira, and their dragons.

"Don't answer them," hissed Silverthief, but Cara shushed her.

"What?"

"We're going exploring!" called Ellis. He held up a piece of parchment, his latest map. "The ruins at the north end. Want to come?"

Cara gazed down, thinking.

Ellis was OK. He loved map-making, and since Cara enjoyed poking around and exploring, they got on quite well. She wasn't sure about Mira. They shared a dorm room, but Mira asked hundreds of questions and Cara liked to keep to herself. They didn't talk much. Now she waited politely. Cara suspected Mira didn't really want her along.

"Um…"

"Come on!" shouted Ellis. "It'll be fun!" He grinned up at her and she smiled despite herself.

"OK."

She leaped down from the roof, with Silverthief following. Ellis's dragon,

DRAGON STORM

Pathseeker, was sturdy and not much larger than Silverthief, and they greeted each other with a friendly sniff. Flameteller, Mira's dragon, pattered back a few steps. He was a nervous thing, and cautious around Silverthief.

Cara and Silverthief

"Where to?" asked Cara.

Ellis led them northwards. "I found some entrances," he said. "I think there are caves underneath this one! I marked them down." He waved his map. "I thought we could explore."

"Ellis said Silverthief is good at finding hidden things," said Mira. "Is that right?"

Cara hesitated and then gave a curt nod.

Mira beamed. "Great! She can help us. And I've invented something!" She held up a strange gadget with a cable and a lamp. "It's so we can send down a light to check. In case we come across any holes." She pushed it towards Cara. "See? We can wind it up and down with this handle!"

Cara shrugged. Mira was fine, she supposed, but her enthusiasm was sometimes very draining.

Silverthief gave a loud, exaggerated sigh, and Mira stopped and looked embarrassed.

Cara tried not to giggle.

Ellis led them through the ruins at the edge of the hall. It was darker here, away from the globes. The ground was thick with weeds and twisted thorn bushes and the remains of ancient streets. Collapsed buildings lay slumped around them.

Cara felt Silverthief tremble with excitement, and grinned. It felt like something new and hidden.

"There!" murmured Ellis.

Tucked half into one of the mounds was an entrance – a square, dark gap that led underground. It looked inviting, but as they got nearer Ellis groaned. A rope was stretched in front of the entrance, and hanging from it was a sign, which read:

THIS AREA
IS OUT OF BOUNDS
FOR SAFETY REASONS
DO NOT
ENTER
Vice Chancellor Creedy

"Rats," said Mira.

Cara scowled. Creedy was Berin's second in command. He was a grim-faced man who taught them dragon riding, and always looked at the children as if there was a bad taste in his mouth.

Silverthief hissed quietly, "*See?*"

Cara frowned. "See what?"

"They're keeping *secrets*," muttered the dragon. "What's down there? What don't they want us to see?"

"It's just for safety," said Cara, but Silverthief shook her head.

"There's something hidden down there. I can *smell* it."

Ellis sighed in frustration. "Well … I

guess that's that."

Cara considered it. "We could go in anyway," she said. "We've got the dragons."

"But the sign says not to," said Mira.

Cara shrugged. "Creedy isn't here – he'll never know, right? Don't you want to see what's down there?"

"Maybe just a *few* steps…" said Ellis doubtfully.

But Mira shook her head. "No, we shouldn't!"

Cara snorted. "Do what you want. *I'm* going in."

She lifted the rope and stepped underneath. Silverthief followed her, and after a moment so did Ellis and Pathseeker, leaving Mira behind.

Cara ignored her. "All right," she said. "Let's *explore*."

EXPLORING

Beyond the entrance, a set of worn stone steps led down into darkness. Pathseeker crept down first, sniffing carefully. Ellis took another lamp from his backpack, lit the candle and held it up, and Cara and Silverthief followed.

The air was cool and smelled of ancient dead leaves. At the bottom of the steps they followed a corridor that turned sharp left after a few yards. The outside light was lost, darkness crowded in, and now there was only the pale circle of light from the lamp, its shadows jumping and swinging as they moved.

"These are really old," murmured Ellis, looking at the walls. Cara realised they were covered in carvings: scenes from battles, images of humans and dragons apparently building something. "I think … *thousands* of years old."

The corridor was long and turned often, rising and falling. Ellis gave Cara the lamp and pulled out more paper, drawing the tunnels as they walked. Ahead of him, Pathseeker muttered things, like: "North by north-west, twenty-five yards, on a one-sixteenth incline," and Ellis scribbled notes. After a while they came to a junction and the tunnel split into two. Ellis peered down both routes.

"Which way?"

"Left," said Silverthief without hesitating. "I can feel something hidden."

Ellis grinned and turned left. Three more times the corridor split, and each time Silverthief gave directions. Lamplight swilled yellow over them. Cara studied the images on the walls as they passed: a lightning bolt, a dragon's wing spread out, a tower, a huge creature with glowing eyes staring down at a crowd of people, a crown, an army going to war...

"Where are we?" she asked.

Ellis peered at his map. "According to this … near the middle of the Guild Hall. But much further down."

"Stop," said Pathseeker suddenly. The children looked up and Cara raised her lamp. Ahead of them the corridor ended suddenly. There was the shape of a doorway but no door within it – just more solid stone wall. There was no keyhole, no door handle. No way through.

"Silver?" asked Cara.

Silverthief came to the front and snuffled around the door frame. "There's a way through," she muttered. "I can *feel* it. But…"

Ellis and Pathseeker waited, and Cara

watched. But as she did so she felt something: a faint draught, like a prickle up the back of her neck. The lamplight seemed to dim.

She lifted the lamp,

checking the

candle, and

noticed that

above the stone

doorway there was an eye.

It was carved into an octagon, like the base of the brooch in the king's room, and it had the same fierce aspect. Before she'd thought it might be from a cat or a wolf; now she knew it was a dragon. But not like Silverthief. This was something cruel, glaring out from the rock. Cara stared at it, her hand trembling, waiting for it to move...

"What are you doing here?" barked a voice.

Ellis and Cara jumped and spun, and the lamp made crazy shadows against the walls. Yellow light suddenly blazed out and blinded them.

Pathseeker staggered and shook her head. Silverthief shimmered into the same colour and pattern as the stone behind her.

The light moved, and Cara reached for her boot knife...

But it was Vice Chancellor Creedy who strode forward and glared at them.

His staff glowed a sick yellow, and it shone

against his pale, dour face.

He looked furious.

"This area is out

of bounds!" he

snapped. "What

do you think

you're doing?"

The children

stared at him, their

hearts pounding.

At last Ellis said,

"Exploring?"

"There was a clear sign!"

snapped Creedy. "The tunnels are

forbidden for *safety* reasons. Leave this area

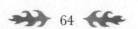

immediately!" He jabbed a finger back down the corridor, and Ellis and Pathseeker meekly headed back.

Silverthief hissed and Cara lifted her chin. "What safety reasons?"

Creedy gave her a look of contempt. "These are ancient ruins, *girl*," he growled. "The tunnels could collapse at any moment! Are you a fool?"

She held his gaze for a few seconds, but he glared back at her and eventually she nodded and followed Ellis back up the corridor.

Silverthief hissed again.

Creedy herded them back to the hut like an angry shepherd driving lost sheep, muttering about foolish children all the way. When they arrived, Berin was waiting for them. Her face was stern but not angry. Next to her, and apparently trying to shrink into the background, was Mira.

"Hello, children," said Berin. "I'm glad you're safe."

Cara said nothing. She glared at Mira, who squirmed.

Berin lifted her hands. "It's not Mira's fault; she did the right thing. She was worried about you." She raised one eyebrow. "After all, you entered an area specifically marked as dangerous."

"We were being careful—" started Ellis.

Cara and Silverthief

"It was perfectly safe!" snapped Cara. "There was nothing wrong down there!"

Berin remained calm. "The tunnels are ancient, Cara, and have been unmapped for centuries. Until we've investigated them we won't know what state they're in, or where a wrong turn might have led you. Trust us on this, hmm?"

She smiled, but Cara looked away.

"Ellis," continued Berin, "I've warned you about your wandering. Exploring is a fine calling, but keep to safe areas, all right?"

He nodded.

"Good," said Berin. "On you go."

Ellis and Mira scurried away. But as Cara turned, Berin said, "Not you, Cara. You and I need to talk."

TRUST
NO ONE

Berin waited until the others had left and then pulled out a chair. "Would you like to sit?"

Cara shook her head.

Berin smiled. "No, you like to be on your feet, don't you? Always ready to run away."

Cara said nothing. It was true. She didn't like to feel trapped, or to have her back to doorways.

Berin sat down herself and looked up.

"So," she said brightly. "Tell me, Cara. How are things?"

Cara frowned. "What do you mean?"

"Well…" Berin waved an arm vaguely. "Are you enjoying life in the Guild? Lessons?"

"S'pose," admitted Cara. "Better than living on the streets."

Berin chuckled. "I imagine! And there's Silverthief, of course. How are things with her? You seem very close."

Cara nodded.

Berin seemed to hesitate. "It's just … I was wondering if you felt you were settling in. I know it's a big change, but the Guild is here for you. *We're* here for you. Are you making friends?"

Cara and Silverthief

Cara shrugged again. "Ellis is OK."

"And the others?"

Cara said nothing. She didn't understand what Berin wanted her to say. She didn't mind the others. She didn't need them either. She had Silverthief.

"We'd like you to feel settled."

Cara frowned again. "You said I could leave when I wanted."

"Well, yes," said Berin, surprised. "But I'd hoped…" She considered Cara for a few moments longer. Eventually she gave a rueful smile, as if she'd played a bad move in a game of chess. "Well. If you want to talk, you can, any time. For now please stay within the safe areas. And … try to relax."

She smiled. "You're safe here, you know."

Cara nodded, and turned and left.

It was the weekend, and many of the children had gone home to see parents or friends. Mira, Ellis and Cara were the only children still there, and dinner was quiet. Mira tried starting a conversation, but Cara ignored her until she fell silent. Ellis nodded amiably, but he was distracted with updating his maps.

That evening, lying in bed, Cara talked to Silverthief.

"I can't believe Mira ratted us out," she whispered, so quietly she hardly even breathed the words.

I know! replied Silverthief at once. *And what was Berin talking about? "Are you making friends?" What's it got to do with her, eh?*

Cara nodded.

And there's something else, said Silverthief. *They're hiding something, I'm sure of it.*

Cara frowned. *"What?"*

Think about it. All those branching tunnels, all those junctions we took. It was like a maze down there, wasn't it?

"So?"

So ... how did Creedy find us so quickly?

Cara blinked. It was true. Mira must have gone back to the Guild to tell Creedy, and he would have had to go through the corridors. But he'd found them almost right away.

"Maybe he heard us?"

Silverthief snorted. *And I saw something else too…*

"What?"

Footprints. There were footprints in the sand, Cara. Someone had been down before us. They went right up to that door … and through it.

Cara stared up at the ceiling, thinking.

We can't trust them, said Silverthief. *There's something they're not telling us. And it's on the other side of that door.*

For the next few days Cara did nothing but watched.

Nothing seemed different. The other children returned, bubbling with excitement and stories and eager to see their dragons again (summoning outside the Guild Hall was strictly forbidden). Creedy continued the riding and flying lessons, wearing his usual scowl. Drun taught them more about summoning and dragon care. And Daisy, the short, round and pink self-defence teacher, trained them in techniques for evading and escaping capture. She was delighted with Cara, and often made her demonstrate to the others, much to Cara's embarrassment.

Cara watched the other children as they talked and laughed, argued and joked. It was strange, the way they went on. It seemed so easy. She wondered what it would be like to join in, but couldn't think what to say.

DRAGON STORM

Another boy joined the group, a blacksmith's son called Tomas, and Cara saw how quickly he settled in. She wondered why she found it so hard. Occasionally someone smiled at her, seemed to be on the edge of inviting her to join them…

Urgh, no, said Silverthief. *They're so annoying!*

Cara ducked her head. It was true. Erin was the worst, with her huge booming laugh, always trying to take over the conversation.

And Connor thinks he's so clever, sneered Silverthief. *And Kai's always asking me about my camouflage; he's really nosy.*

Cara nodded. Silverthief was right, of course. But … Ellis was nice. Exploring had been … fun? She wondered if she should tell him about Creedy.

We can't trust him. He'll just tell a grown-up, like Mira did.

Cara wasn't sure about that, but Silverthief's voice was firm.

We can't trust any of them, Cara. There's just us. We have to solve this together.

In the evenings she didn't join in the conversations with Erin and Mira. She just sat on her bunk with her back against the wall, completely still, like she used to when she was on the streets. She sat until she seemed to fade away, until the others stopped noticing her, stopped even thinking about her. At night, when the others slept, she crept up on to the roof and watched the hall, enjoying the silence. Occasionally she saw people moving around. But they didn't see her.

One time, she saw Tomas leave. He looked sad, and she wondered if, perhaps, he'd also found it hard to fit in. Silverthief told her that Tomas couldn't hold the connection with his own dragon, Ironskin.

That means he's not a proper dragonseer, she said, rather gleefully.

But a few days later he returned and seemed much happier, and suddenly Ironskin could stay with him for as long as she wanted. *And* Ironskin had developed her special power – Protection magic – and she was now able to create a shield around herself and others. Cara didn't know what had happened and felt too awkward to ask. She wondered what Silverthief's powers would be.

Often, Cara noticed Creedy moving around. He would creep out of the Guild Hall and return an hour later, or more; sometimes Cara fell asleep before he returned. She wondered what he was up to.

One evening, he didn't go outside. Instead he peered around carefully, and

then strode northwards towards the ruins
and the entrance Ellis had discovered.

Cara slipped silently down from the roof
and followed him.

SECRETS

The world was dark. The globes that hung from the roof were now as dim and faint as stars, and everything was shadow. Cara followed Vice Chancellor Creedy as he hurried towards the north end of the hall and the entrance that led underground.

Creedy slipped under the warning rope and down the steps. Cara crept closer and peered inside. As she did, a faint yellow light appeared, and she saw Creedy's face in the glow of his staff. His expression was serious.

I knew it! hissed Silverthief in her mind.

Cara nodded and slunk down the steps after him.

She had no lamp or matches, and wouldn't have dared to light them anyway, but her night vision was good. Carefully, staying just behind the light, she followed Creedy. He was going the same way as before, and at each split in the tunnels he turned without stopping. Silverthief had been right, she realised – Creedy knew exactly where he was going.

At the last turning Cara paused. She could hear something from round the corner – a faint scraping sound. She took a deep breath and poked her head round.

Cara and Silverthief

The vice chancellor was standing at the stone wall the children had reached and seemed to be drawing a pattern on it in chalk. The pattern was complex and twirling, and at its heart was an eye inside an octagon. He muttered as he drew. Then he finished, put the chalk away and pressed against the door …

… and it slid open.

A magic lock, murmured Silverthief. *That's why I couldn't find it!*

Creedy stepped through, and a few seconds later Cara followed him. The corridor beyond had walls of smooth white stone and white sand underfoot. A dim red light came from a doorway at the far end. She crept forward and peered inside.

It was a wide, tall chamber. The ceiling was covered in jewels that glowed with a strange red light. At the far wall there was another doorway, perhaps leading to more corridors. Inside she could see a sarcophagus, an ancient stone coffin. Standing on top was a statue of a woman with a powerful, rather stern expression.

Creedy was standing next to the coffin. He was closer than she'd expected, and facing to one side – if he turned his head a fraction, he would see her! Cara froze, but she didn't gasp. She didn't make any sound at all. She concentrated on breathing silently, and tried to let herself become invisible and melt into the wall behind her.

Creedy didn't notice her. He was looking up at something Cara couldn't see. He seemed nervous, she thought, and his face was pale.

"You must understand," he said. "The importance of this—"

There was a reply, low and fierce.

"*Let. Me. Go.*"

Cara and Silverthief

There was someone else in the room! The voice was old and tired, but burned with anger.

Creedy shook his head. "You know the deal. If you want me to set you free, give me the jewel."

"But it's *mine*!"

Set you free? wondered Cara. Who was this person? Was Creedy keeping them *prisoner*? She strained forward, trying to see. She could make out faint lines in the air, like a barrier. The lines were pale yellow, like the glow of Creedy's staff, and they fizzed with a sound like a crackling fire. Cara stretched a little further…

Sand scrunched under her foot and Creedy turned. Cara pulled back like a snake.

"Hello?" called Creedy sharply.

Oh no! whispered Silverthief's voice. *Go now, Cara!*

Cara crept back up the corridor, trying to move quickly and silently.

"Is someone there?"

Creedy's voice was closer now. He was coming! She turned and raced away, the sand tugging at her feet. Round the corner, and the next, into almost pitch black. Behind her she heard footsteps and saw yellow light swing to and fro as the vice chancellor ran up the corridor after her.

"Show yourself!" he bellowed. "Who are you? Stop!"

A PLAN

Cara raced through the stone doorway and down the corridor, bouncing against the walls in the darkness. Creedy had the light from his staff to guide him, and he was gaining on her. She reached a junction, and another, scrambling to get out. But even if she made it to the entrance, he would see her, she realised. What could she do?

She skidded to a halt.

What are you doing? came Silverthief's voice.

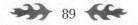

Cara ignored her and backed up the corridor to the last junction. Then she crept a few steps up the other path and crouched low in the darkness. The light came nearer, and she watched as Creedy hurried past and towards the entrance.

She heard his feet pounding, and then silence. She waited in the dark, not daring to move. Had he really left? Or was he waiting for her? Would he come back? But at last she crept back to the junction and listened. Nothing.

She checked the stone doorway but it was closed again. The vice chancellor must have shut it behind him as he chased her. She summoned Silverthief, and the little dragon snuffled around the frame. "No," she said at last. "It's magic, Cara. I can't get through this."

Cara nodded and they made their way to the entrance. She listened again, but Creedy wasn't there. He must have run all the way back to the Guild buildings, looking for her. She breathed a sigh of relief, left the tunnels and crept back to the dorm. The globes were already starting to glow brighter as she closed her eyes in bed, creating a fake dawn.

Her mind whirred. Who was the prisoner? What was the jewel Creedy wanted? Had he seen her? Who could she tell?

No one, whispered Silverthief. *We can't trust anyone.*

Cara fell into a fitful sleep and awoke an hour later, bleary and confused, to another morning.

Vice Chancellor Creedy was lying. He'd told the children that the tunnels were closed for safety reasons, but that wasn't it at all. He was keeping someone a prisoner, and demanding something in return for letting them go. Did Berin know too?

She must, said Silverthief. *Creedy is her second in command!*

"Who can we tell then?"

No one.

They had Drun for dragon care that day. All the dragons were there – huge Rockhammer

bending over Erin; wily Lightspirit talking with Connor; Ellis and the odd stumpy Pathseeker. Mira was there with Flameteller, the strange angular creature who looked almost like a model of bronze and wood, and Tomas with Ironskin, her dark-red skin streaked in orange lines of fire. Kai was stroking Boneshadow, the white dragon with a red flare on her chest.

Ellis gave Cara a friendly wave, and she nodded.

"Maybe we could tell the others," she murmured.

Ha! said Silverthief scornfully. *Like Mira? She'd just tell the adults!*

"Ellis?"

Silverthief said nothing. *Perhaps Ellis,* thought Cara. *Tomas seems all right...*

The only ones we can trust are each other, insisted Silverthief. *That's how it's always been.* Then Silverthief added, *But that gives me an idea.*

Cara listened. She wasn't sure she liked it, but Silverthief was right – it might work...

After lunch, she found Ellis alone in the hut. He was working on his maps, and when Cara entered he glanced up and smiled.

"Hello! Look!"

He showed her his latest drafts, and Cara nodded, impressed. They were very

Cara and Silverthief

detailed, showing all the parts of the hall, with areas marked off "For exploring". She saw the ruins to the north with the entrance.

"I'd love to investigate that area some more," said Ellis. "Maybe when it's safe, eh?"

"Maybe," said Cara. She looked at his piles of rough copies and pulled out another. "What's this?"

Ellis grinned. "That's the west of the city!" he said. "It's one of the first maps I ever

made. I spent two days exploring every street in the whole of the west quarter. I had to ask my big brother to come with me; cost me four weeks' pocket money. But isn't it good? There, that's Needle Street. Did you know there used to be a river under there?"

He chatted and pointed, moving over to the hut window to get more light, and Cara asked him questions. But as she talked she casually reached back, pulled one particular map from the pile, and slipped it down between two desks.

She felt bad – she really did like Ellis – but Silverthief was right. The only people they could trust were each other, and she had to know what was going on.

After dinner, she crept into the hut and retrieved the map and headed back towards the ruins. It would be better to wait until darkness, but it wouldn't take Ellis long to notice one of his maps was missing. She checked the map as she walked, trying to memorise it.

The route in was blocked; the magical door sealed solid. But there was another way, wasn't there? She'd seen another door, on the other side of the chamber. And Ellis had said that he'd found other entrances into the tunnels...

She searched the map and its tiny detailed comments, and found it. Another way in –

an entrance that perhaps even Creedy didn't know about. But Cara would find it, and if it wasn't magically locked…

She would learn the truth.

THE
PRISONER

The second entrance was right where Ellis's map said it would be, near a cluster of ruins right against the Guild Hall walls. Cara felt guilty again about stealing his map, but pushed the thought away. This was important. Creedy was lying. Perhaps Berin too. What were they up to really? What were they planning?

At the entrance she reached in her pack for a dark lantern, a small lamp with a sliding cover. She lit it, opened the cover enough to let out just a tiny glimmer of light, and crept down the ancient steps. It was like the other entrance, but the roof had caved in at the bottom. There was only a narrow gap, too small for an adult. Cara squeezed through and into the tunnels.

She summoned Silverthief, and the dragon whispered into existence.

"Ready?" she asked.

Silverthief sniffed and nodded. "This way," she growled.

Cara felt a thrill run up her spine. It was always there, before a mission, that feeling. When the world was against you, when it was just you and your wits, and perhaps one good

friend you trusted more than anyone else.
The thrill that led her to climb sheer walls,
to rob the king, to make things deliberately
hard for herself…

"Let's go," she whispered, and they
ventured into the dark.

The tunnel twisted and branched, and
Silverthief led her without hesitating. Cara
checked the dusty floor but saw no footprints.
No one had come this way for decades,
perhaps centuries. Her lamp sent a tiny point
of light out into the darkness, and picked out
more pictures on the walls. Carvings, spots
of ancient red paint. A crown, a sword, a
city on fire…

"Here," whispered Silverthief, and Cara

realised they were at a stone doorway like the other one. Another angry stone eye glared at her from above. Her heart sank, but Silverthief seemed excited.

"No magic," she muttered. "It's not protected. I can sense… Ah." She lifted one claw and pushed at an exact point on the door, and the door swung inwards a few inches and stuck. Cara and the dragon heaved it open and squeezed through.

White sand hissed under Cara's feet and the air glowed faintly red. She closed her lantern and crept down the tunnel. There was no sound. She moved closer…

The tunnel opened out into the chamber. On the far side was the doorway where

Creedy had entered. Red jewels glowed above, and there was the sarcophagus, the stone coffin with the statue of the woman standing on top. On the other side of the chamber, pale-yellow lines glowed in circles, one on top of the other, forming an enormous cage.

Inside the cage was a dragon.

He seemed to be asleep, his snout resting on his two front legs and his long tail curled round himself. He was large, perhaps as big as Erin's dragon, Rockhammer, and soft green, mottled and streaked. His tail and snout were tinged with grey, and the dragon's skin seemed stretched. He looked very old, Cara thought.

Cara and Silverthief

Cara stared and listened to his gentle snoring. A *dragon*. Creedy was keeping a *dragon* prisoner!

"I was right!" hissed Silverthief. "They're up to no good!"

Cara nodded. She turned and walked over to the statue. It was ancient and coated in a thick layer of dust, but she could see it was a woman with long robes and a circlet over her head almost like a crown. She was holding a stone sword in one hand. Round her neck was an emerald set into an eight-sided stone brooch.

Was this the jewel Creedy had wanted? But then why hadn't he just taken it? Cara turned back to the dragon and stopped.

His eyes were open, and he was watching her.

JADEHEART

The dragon didn't move at first. Slowly he examined Cara from top to bottom. Then he lifted his head, stood, and *stretched*, arching his back like a cat. Cara saw that round his neck hung a much larger necklace, with a huge emerald. He extended his front claws until they almost touched the yellow bars of his cage.

"You're new," he said in a thick, low growl. "Are you with *him*?"

Cara stared. "Um … who?"

The dragon sneered. "*Him. Creedy*. Are you working with him?"

"No." Cara shook her head. "He doesn't know I'm here. Did he capture you? Did he do this?" She waved at the lines that made a cage around him, and he nodded.

He peered at Cara. "Why are you here then?"

"I followed him," said Cara. "Before. What's he doing? Why has he got you here?"

She had a sudden thought. Dragons needed humans to summon them, and to keep the connection that allowed them to stay. But they could leave at any time. Why was this dragon staying in his cage? Why not return to his own world?

"Where's your human?" she asked.

The dragon looked at her, and his face was so sad that Cara felt terrible. She looked at the stone effigy. "Oh," she said softly. "Is that … her?"

The other dragon nodded. "Tanora. She was my human, long ago. Long … long ago." He nodded again. "I am Jadeheart."

"Cara," said Cara. "And Silverthief."

The dragons nodded to each other.

"I don't understand," said Silverthief. "How can you still be here, in this world?"

Jadeheart shrugged. "I am loyal." He tried to peer across towards the statue.

Cara realised that from within his cage he couldn't quite see it.

"What does Creedy want?" asked Silverthief.

Jadeheart tapped the jewel. "This." He gave a sad smile. "A small thing. But it is everything I have, and everything I am."

He sighed. "It was long ago now," he murmured. "But once, Tanora and I lived, and we were never apart. She was my human, and I was her dragon."

Cara smiled. "Like me and Silverthief." Silverthief purred.

"Perhaps," said Jadeheart. "She was a mighty warrior and a magician, and I was a king among dragons." His eyes looked misty. "I loved to fly, to carry her into battle – and there were so many battles! It was a fearsome time. The time of the Dragon Storm, when humans and dragons fought to save the land – and none fought harder than Tanora and Jadeheart!

"We were inseparable. We swore never to be apart, and Tanora created her greatest magic – she took the bond between us and sealed it, forever, into this jewel. No matter what happened, I would stay in this world with Tanora, forever!

"But –" he scowled – "we were betrayed. Tanora was wounded. She did not recover."

He swung his head in a sad arc. "They

buried her here, in this crypt … and I stayed with her."

Cara looked around the chamber. "For a thousand years?" she breathed.

"Until *that human* found me." The dragon's lip curled. "Oh, he was so *friendly* – 'Oh, great dragon, how *amazing* you are!' But he saw my jewel … and he *wanted* it."

Jadeheart waved a paw. "'Only a look,' he said, but I saw his face. He meant to keep it. He wanted it for himself."

"So he made you a prisoner?" said Silverthief.

"He said he would let me go if I gave up the jewel. But if I do, I will fall from this world and lose Tanora. And if I do not –"

the dragon reached a claw out towards the crackling yellow lines, and sparks flew up – "I will be trapped forever."

Silverthief hissed like an angry cat, and her skin almost glowed in fury. "How could he do this? It's *awful*!"

"We should tell Berin," said Cara.

"Unless Berin already knows. Unless they're working together!"

Cara chewed her lip. "Yes…"

"Please help me," said Jadeheart. "I just want to see my human's face again."

Cara studied the shimmering cage. "How?"

Silverthief sniffed. "This is powerful magic," she said. "It needs an anchor.

Something … *hidden*." She looked around. "Something to hold it into place somewhere…"

Cara stared down at the scuffed earth around the cage, and dug through the sand until she felt something, slender and strong. It was silver, woven into a thin rope.

"This is it!" she exclaimed. Then she stopped. "Do you hear something?"

Silverthief's ears pricked and Cara listened. There was something very faint… The sound of footsteps, hurrying towards them. It was hard to tell from which direction—

"Creedy!" hissed Silverthief. "He's on his way!"

Cara and Silverthief

"Quickly!" said Jadeheart. "Please!"

Cara nodded, lifted the rope, and pulled it apart. There was a noise like a *crack* and the yellow lines flared and seemed to widen. They turned as pale as ghosts and passed right through Cara and Silverthief, and the girl and dragon flinched, but all they felt was

a strange tingle … and then they were gone.

Jadeheart stretched again. "Ah… Oh, *thank you.*" He bounded to the coffin and gazed at the statue again. "Oh, Tanora…"

"We can go back up the other tunnel," said Cara. "Quick, before he gets here!"

Jadeheart stayed leaning over the sarcophagus, crooning a sad song.

"Jadeheart!" called Cara. "He's coming!"

Jadeheart growled. "Let him come," he hissed. "This time I'll be ready."

Cara and Silverthief swapped worried looks.

"I don't know if that's a good idea,"

said Silverthief. "Why don't we just slip away?"

The green dragon bowed his head. "Hmm," he said thoughtfully. "Hmm."

Then he made a sound, almost like a chuckle.

"I know what you're trying to do," he said. "Do you think I'm a fool?"

Cara blinked. "Er … what?"

"I know what you really want," hissed Jadeheart. "Oh yes. I know what you want, Silver*thief.*" He reared up and glared at them. "You want the jewel for yourselves, don't you? You want to take me away from my human!"

Cara gaped. "No!" she managed.

"Really, Jadeheart. You can trust us."

She reached out and patted the dragon's shoulder, and it sighed. Then it swung one paw *fast*, caught Cara – and flung her hard against the wall!

FRIENDS

Cara twisted as she hurtled through the air, and managed to get her feet up to cushion the blow, but still she was winded. Behind her, Silverthief rushed at Jadeheart, but he batted her away like a toy. He stood at his full height, ferocious, with lines of power radiating off him. He seemed to be growing.

"*Thieves!*" he screamed. "Thieves, come to take my jewel! Come to take my *human!*"

"We're not," croaked Cara, trying to get

her breath back. "Jadeheart, you can trust us—"

"I can't trust *any* of you!" he roared. "I can't trust anyone but Tanora! I trusted her and she trusted me! We don't need anyone else!"

Now the lines around him were like waves of fire, flattening Cara against the wall. And the walls themselves glowed green, mixing horribly with the red light. Across the chamber, Silverthief picked herself up and shook her head.

"Silver!" shouted Cara. "We have to get out of here!"

Jadeheart's eyes shone with mad fury. "Oh no you don't!" he roared. "Thieves must be *punished*!"

He took a deep breath and ROARED. The flames grew even higher.

"You want to split us apart!" he screamed. "You're like all the others!"

"We're not!" yelled Cara. "I promise!"

"Liars!"

He swung his tail around in a high crashing arc, and Cara dodged it.

"Villains!"

"CARA!" roared a voice, and Cara spun and stared as Ellis and Pathseeker came crashing into the chamber.

"*Ellis?*"

"Cara, what's going on?" Ellis bellowed. Behind him were Mira and Flameteller, and Tomas and Ironskin!

DRAGON STORM

"More of you?" spat Jadeheart. "Come to attack me! Come to steal my jewel!"

"Watch out!" shouted Cara, as the huge green dragon drew a breath and ROARED again. Green flames shot out and over Ellis, and Cara covered her mouth in horror.

"Ellis!"

But to her astonishment, the flames didn't touch him. And now she saw Ironskin's face fixed in concentration and she remembered – this was Ironskin's special power, to create a shield! The green flames blistered against it but couldn't get through.

Cara turned back to Jadeheart and noticed the jewel again. It was pulsing horribly. Jadeheart grew larger with every pulse, as if feeding off it – but somehow it seemed to be feeding off him too.

"Jadeheart!" she shouted. "I think the jewel is doing something to you!"

"*Lies.*"

"We're dragonseers, Jadeheart! We're like Tanora! Trust us!"

Jadeheart shifted between Cara and the other children, as if deciding who to attack first. He brought his tail round in a mighty sweep and it crashed into the others, driving them away from the doorway, and he bellowed again.

"Cara!" hissed Silverthief. "We can go!"

Cara gaped. "What?"

"Look! We can make it out!" Cara turned and saw what she meant. Jadeheart was distracted by the other children, who were now halfway round the chamber, away from the doorway. There was a gap!

"But what about the others?"

"That great lout Ironskin has her magic shield; they'll be fine," said Silverthief.

Cara and Silverthief

"Come on!"

She shoved Cara towards the doorway and they dived out. Cara turned back for a moment and watched Jadeheart's flames attacking Ironskin's shield. It was still holding. The other dragons, Pathseeker and Flameteller, seemed to be trying to talk to Jadeheart, without much success.

"Come *on*!" hissed Silverthief.

Cara stumbled down the corridor. "Why was Ellis there?" she panted. "And Tom and Mira?"

Silverthief snorted. "Who cares? All that matters is you and me!"

The exit was ahead, its dim light gleaming. This close to the edge of the hall the globes were sparse and dim. Hardly anyone came out this far. No wonder only Ellis had discovered about the second entrance.

Cara stopped running. "*That's* why they're here," she muttered. "Ellis must have noticed we took the map."

Silverthief said, "So he wanted it back, eh? Didn't want you exploring! Typical!"

"No," said Cara. "I mean, I think he came for me... Silver, I think they came to rescue us!"

"What?" hissed the dragon, baffled. "Why would they do *that*? Come on!"

But Cara stood still. "They came to get us," she said stubbornly. "They thought we might get into trouble, and they came to rescue us. They were… Ellis is…" She hesitated. "Silver, I think Ellis is my friend."

"What?!" Now the silvery dragon looked furious. "Cara, *I'm* your friend!"

"Yes, of course! But maybe Ellis is too?"

Silverthief shook her head. "No, no. It's you and me, Cara. It always has been! The only people we can trust are each other!"

Cara looked at her. "Yes," she said. And then: "No. That's what Jadeheart said. That's what he said about his human, but he's *wrong*. Don't you understand?"

Silverthief stared at her with a baffled expression. "No. I can't…"

"Yes," said Cara firmly. "Yes, Silver. Look. You trust me, yes?"

"Yes, always!"

"Then trust me now. Ellis is ... *our friend*. Mira is our friend. Tom is our friend. They invited us to go exploring. Ellis showed me the maps. They came to *rescue* us. They're our *friends*!"

She gasped. "And we've left them in danger!"

She spun and ran back down the corridor, towards the chamber and the shouting.

"Wait!" cried Silverthief, but Cara ignored her. "Cara, wait!"

POWERS

Cara burst back into the chamber and threw her hands up against her face. The flames were worse than ever! In the centre, Jadeheart was howling and shrieking and throwing balls of green fire at the other children and dragons. He'd blocked off their escape, and now they were huddled under Ironskin's magical shield. Flameteller and Pathseeker kept darting out, trying to talk to Jadeheart, or distract him, but with no luck.

DRAGON STORM

"Thieves!" howled Jadeheart. "Traitors!"

He seemed unaware of Cara, and she tried to work out what to do. Distract him? But then what? He was growing even larger, and at his breast the jewel glowed a sick bright green, thrumming with power.

The jewel…

She had to get the jewel. She looked at Jadeheart's hide, covered in rough scales. Could she climb up the tail? It was insane but she didn't know what else to do. She took a deep breath, got ready to run—

Something crashed down on her back and she collapsed to the floor. She spun and stared up into the eyes of Silverthief. The dragon's face was furious and confused.

Cara and Silverthief

"What are you *doing*?" Silverthief hissed.

"Trying to get the jewel! It's where his power comes from!"

"It's too risky! You could get hurt!" Silverthief looked as if she was about to cry. "Why are you doing this, Cara? Why are you doing this to me? To us?"

Ironskin's shield was weakening. There was so little time! But Cara tried to stay calm. She looked into Silverthief's eyes and spoke as gently as she could.

"Silver, they're our *friends*. We're not used to that, but they are. I trust you. You trust me. *We can trust them*. And they're in trouble. We have to help." She smiled. "It's what friends do."

Silverthief shook her head. For a moment she seemed about to howl. But then she sighed.

"But … then … are *we* still friends?"

Cara hugged the dragon tight round her neck. "Silver, you're the best friend I could ever have!"

Silverthief sighed again. "Well. Well, good." She almost looked embarrassed. Then her eyes widened. "Wait – I can feel what to do!"

She stood up and closed her eyes. She began to sway slightly.

"Silver?"

"Shh!"

Silverthief's skin was a mix of red and

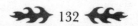

green, matching the colours around her. But now she seemed fainter. Fainter… Suddenly Cara realised she wasn't seeing Silverthief at all – she was seeing *through* her! The dragon was disappearing, becoming invisible, until only the faint silver glow of her edges remained.

Cara reached out to touch Silverthief and gasped. Her own hand was the same! She could see through it to the ground below. It was faintly white, like a ghost, and getting paler and paler…

"Is this your power?" she breathed.

"I think so. I think I can do it for me, and for you too." The faint outline of her face grinned. "Come on – let's be heroes!"

Cara leaped on to Silverthief's back. It was a weird sensation, as if she was sitting on nothing. And then it got much worse, as Silverthief took a few steps and launched herself into the air. Cara clung to an invisible neck and tried not to look down. Heights didn't bother her but this was something else!

"I'll get as close as I can," muttered Silverthief, and flew round to the front of Jadeheart, avoiding his huge green claws. She wasn't a very good flyer, and lurched from side to side. Cara held on desperately.

"Ready?" hissed Silverthief. "You'll have to jump!"

Cara gulped, lifted her feet and crouched on Silverthief's back. One … two…

Three!

She leaped forward and caught hold of the huge silver necklace by one hand, dangling down.

Jadeheart peered down. "Who's that?"

Cara was still invisible but Jadeheart could feel her. One claw swung round and Cara lurched to the side, still holding the chain. She scrambled for the jewel.

There it was – an eight-sided silver brooch with a lurid green stone glowing inside. Cara wasn't sure what to do next. The chain was as thick as her wrist, heavy and solid. The brooch looked secure.

"Watch out!" shouted Silverthief, and Cara swung again as another claw battered at her.

"Who's there?!" roared Jadeheart again. "Thief! I can *feel* you!"

There was only one thing to do.

"I'm sorry," whispered Cara. She whipped her knife out from her boot, flipped it round and smashed its base against the jewel.

She wasn't sure what she expected. She hoped she would knock the jewel out of its setting. But to her surprise the emerald shattered at once. It had seemed strong, but inside it was rotten. The green flames around them collapsed, and Jadeheart gasped.

"Nooooo!"

He staggered and seemed to shrink. Cara swung madly on the chain by one hand, and then leaped, curled, and landed in a crouch.

"Cara!" shouted Silverthief.

Cara held up a hand. "I'm OK," she gasped, before turning to Jadeheart.

Already the dragon was back to the size he'd been when Cara had first found him. He was scrabbling around at the floor of the chamber, trying to scrape together the tiny pieces of shattered jewel and making a horrible sad wail.

Cara walked towards him.

"Stay back!" warned Silverthief, but she kept going.

Now Jadeheart was only as big as Ironskin.

"Tanora," he mumbled. "Tanora!" He stumbled over to the tomb and gazed down.

"I'm sorry," whispered Cara. Awkwardly she reached up and patted the creature's flanks.

The dragon sobbed. "It wasn't the same, you know. After she was gone. The jewel reminded me of her. But it wasn't the same. It…" He looked surprised. "Oh, I attacked you all! Oh dear!"

"It was the jewel," said Cara. "It wasn't you."

"Tanora wouldn't have wanted that," he

mumbled. Now he was only a little taller than Cara.

"It's OK," said Cara. "She'll understand."

Jadeheart sniffed. "What will happen now?"

The other dragons limped forward.

"You'll return to our world," said Flameteller.

Jadeheart frowned. "It's been so long…" he murmured.

Pathseeker smiled. "It's easy," she said. "We'll come with you and show you the way."

Ironskin said, "And then you can dream."

Jadeheart looked up hopefully. "Will I … remember her?"

"Always," said Silverthief. "She was your best friend, and you were hers. You'll remember her forever."

Jadeheart sighed. He was fading now. "I'd like that," he murmured. "I'd like…"

And then he was gone, and the other dragons too, and the chamber was silent.

FAMILY

The children squeezed back through the hole at the bottom of the entrance and up to the surface.

"Uh-oh," murmured Ellis.

Cara looked up and groaned. Creedy was stalking towards them, his staff held up high and yellow light flaring off it, his face furious. Behind him was Berin.

Creedy glared at them. "And just what do you think you're doing here?" he demanded.

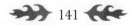

The children looked at each other. Cara realised they were a mess – their hair singed, their clothes torn and burnt, their hands scratched and sooty.

"Exploring?" said Ellis tentatively.

Creedy bristled. "Didn't I give strict instructions—"

"It's not their fault," said Cara. "It's mine. I went … exploring, and got into trouble."

Now Berin was with them. She examined them carefully. "Is everyone all right?"

"Oh yes," said Cara, and smiled. "My friends rescued me."

There was a lot of shouting. A *lot*. First, Creedy shouted at them all for a while. Then he went to explore the chamber and Berin spoke to them in a serious, disappointed voice, until Cara thought she would prefer to be shouted at. And then Creedy came back from the chamber and *did* shout at them again, for even longer this time.

And then finally they were sent off to Hilda, the matron and cook for their hut. She clucked over their scratches, gave them buckets of hot water to wash with, and served them slices of bread straight from the oven with butter and new jam, and sent them off to bed.

The next day, Cara was summoned to Berin's office. When she got there, Berin was waiting, and Malik too. He nodded to her but his face looked unusually serious.

Berin sat. Cara stood.

"Vice Chancellor Creedy has given me his report," said Berin. "It appears he found the chamber some weeks ago, and Jadeheart too."

"He kept him prisoner," said Cara.

Berin pursed her lips. "The vice chancellor says that Jadeheart became violent and had to be restrained. He was trying to get Jadeheart to hand over the jewel voluntarily. He thought this might be better."

Cara said nothing. Berin sighed. "Tanora and Jadeheart were heroes once, you know," she said softly. "Legends, even. They fought in the Dragon Storm war and saved many lives. They were inseparable. Their link was so strong, Jadeheart lived almost entirely in this world.

"The jewel was well meant, but it changed them both. Towards the end, Tanora was … different. And poor Jadeheart too."

Cara said, "When I smashed the jewel, he seemed to change."

"Hmm. Is there anything else I should know?"

Cara hesitated.

Should we tell them? said Silverthief's voice in her mind. *We might get into trouble…*

Cara took a deep breath. "Well … when I met Malik … at the palace—"

"While you were *robbing* the palace," said Berin in a level voice.

145

Cara coughed. "Um … yeah. The thing is, there was this rumour going around downtown, about the king. About this special jewel he had, worth more than the entire kingdom. I mean, that's what folk said."

Berin gazed at Cara.

"So, um, that's what I was there for," said Cara. "And I found it. I didn't take it! But … it was like the jewel Jadeheart had. Only it wasn't green; it was a diamond. But it had eight sides. And there was a…" She hesitated. "An *eye* in it. Like, a *real eye*. It moved."

Berin and Malik stared at her.

"King Godfic has a Dragon's Eye," murmured Malik. He whistled. "Now, *that's* interesting."

Berin nodded. "Thank you, Cara. Anything else?"

Cara shook her head.

"Right." Berin studied her. "Well, Malik is here to take you back to the city. So, thank you for spending time with us, and good luck with your life."

Cara started. "What?"

Berin looked surprised. "Well, that's what you want, isn't it? To leave?"

She sighed. "Cara, you broke the rules, more than once. You put the others in danger. You *stole* from Ellis. And … you just don't seem to be happy here.

"This isn't a prison, you know. You can leave. Malik will help. We can give you a little money, or find you a foster home – a good home, with good people. It's up to you. You can leave whenever you want."

She studied Cara. "*Is* that what you want?"

We could leave, said Silverthief. *We could leave, Cara!*

Cara said nothing.

I mean, that would be best, wouldn't it? Silverthief's voice wasn't quite so certain as usual. *I mean … I suppose Pathseeker is all right. And Ironskin's Protection magic was good. But we don't need them. Flameteller's quite nice when you get to know him. But, I mean…* She trailed off.

Cara said slowly, "Would it be all right if I … if I stayed here? Perhaps a bit longer?"

Berin raised an eyebrow. "Oh?"

"Well…" said Cara awkwardly. "I mean, my friends are here."

Berin looked back down at her paperwork. "Of course," she said.

Cara nodded. That seemed to be it. She turned to leave.

"Oh, Cara?" said Berin.

Cara turned back.

Berin smiled. "Welcome to the family."

Have you read the first

book in the series,

TOMAS AND IRONSKIN?

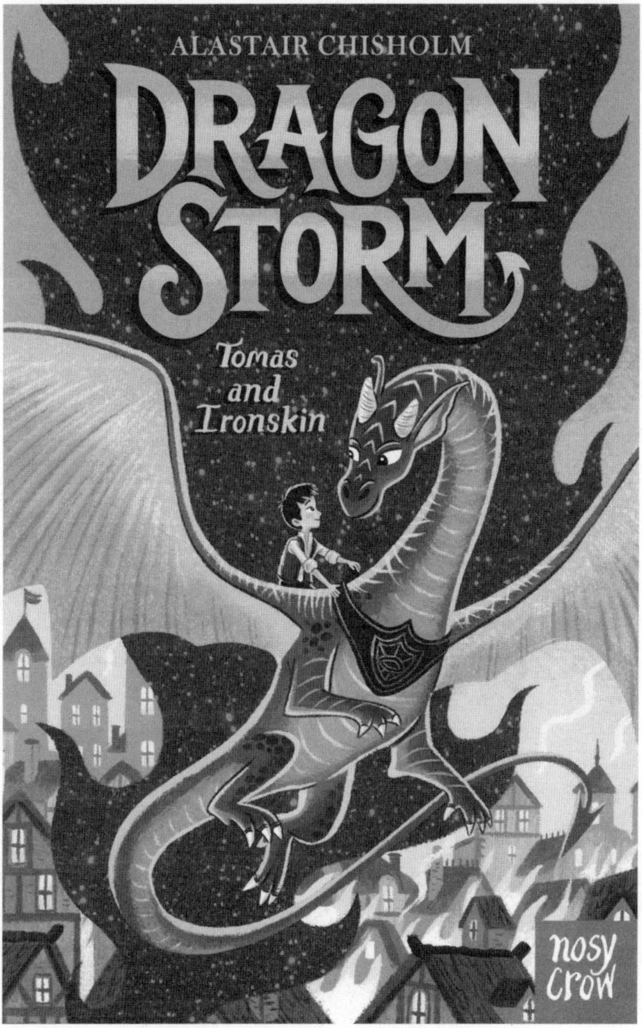
ALASTAIR CHISHOLM
DRAGON STORM
Tomas and Ironskin
nosy crow

Look out for more books in
the Dragon Storm series:

ELLIS AND PATHSEEKER

MIRA AND FLAMETELLER

KAI AND BONESHADOW

ERIN AND ROCKHAMMER